Harry Potter

AND THE CHAMBER OF SECRETS

SCHOLASTIC INC.

New York   Toronto   London   Auckland   Sydney
Mexico City   New Delhi   Hong Kong   Buenos Aires

1/29/22

hi. We went to GG's house and I had a little bit of fun, we went there for liv's bday party. liv got loads of gifts and I was happy for her. Love katie

1/30/22

hi.
We
Went
snow
tubing
today
and
I
had
a blast
there but at the end my
feet were wet and cold
so when we got home
daddy said i could turn on his
space heater. Love, katie

Hi today is olivia's bday
and We had to go to school
I had a olk day at school.
In music
We did

the boom
Wackers
and Sang
encanto songs
So I had fun

doing that. Love,
Katie

1/31/22

2/1/22

hi. Today is
the first day
of febuary
and its
almost
Valintines
day.
ms
nicole
started
putting
up
the
Hearts
and tels as Why she Loves
as. Love Katie

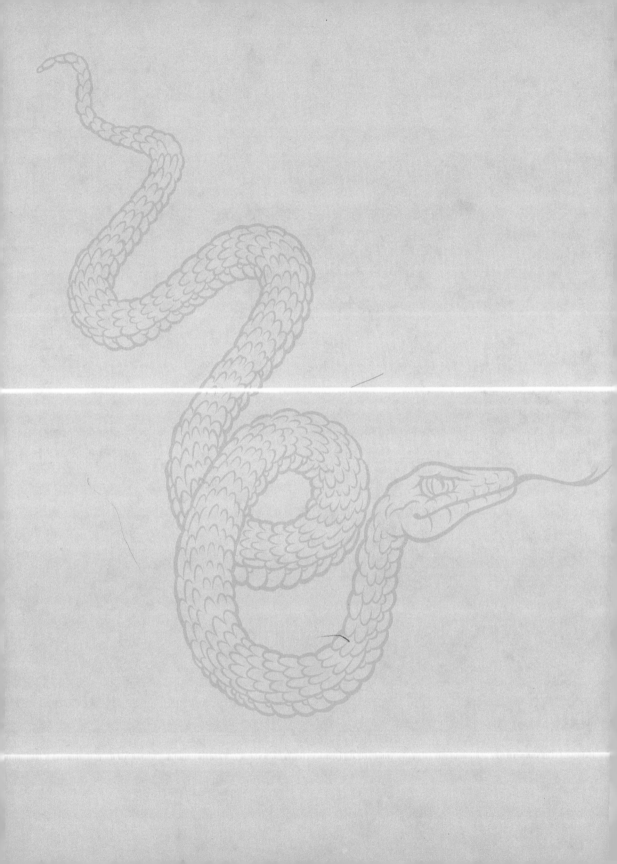

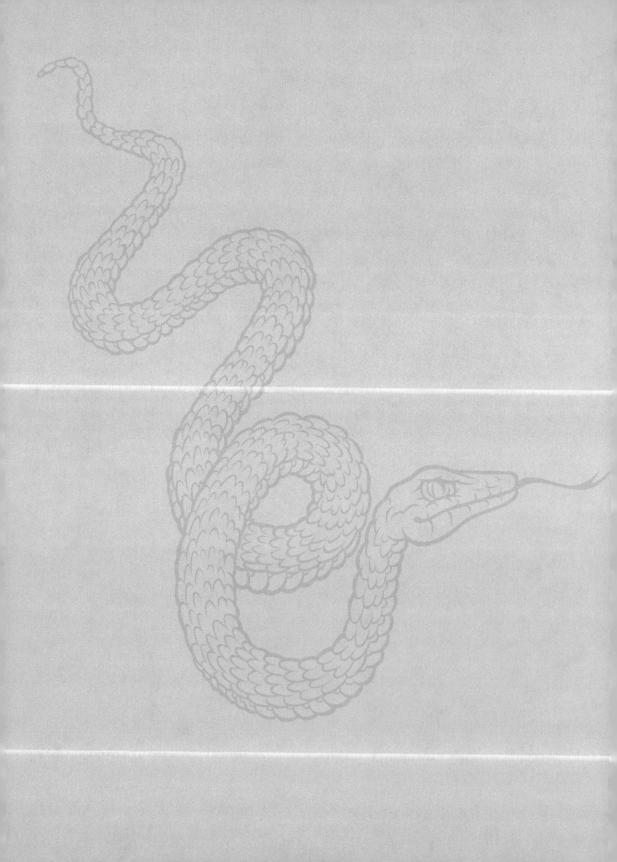

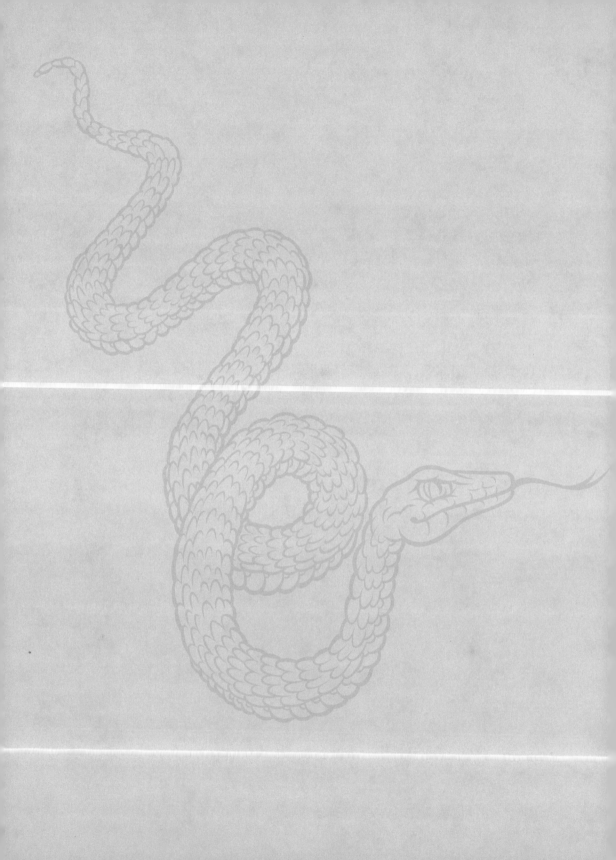

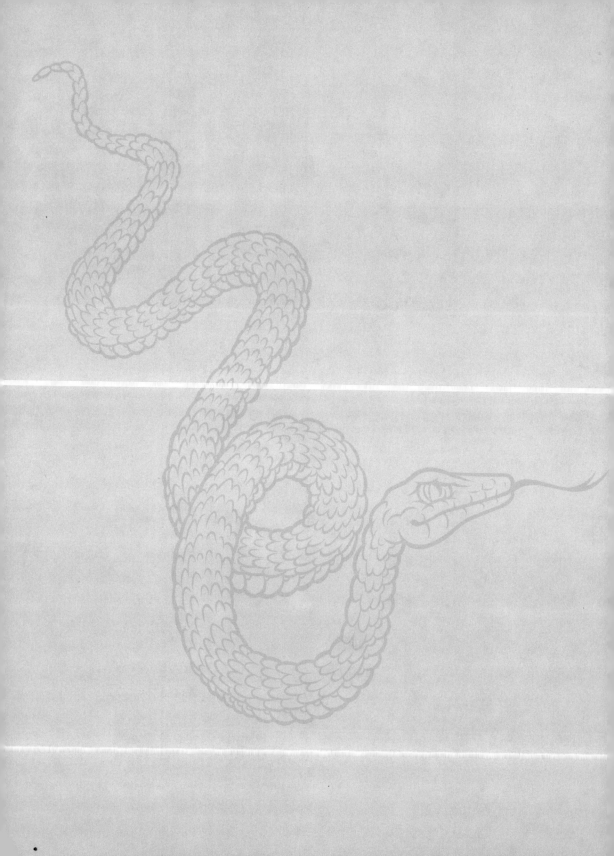

powdered
horn of
B'CORN